SMART IS THE NEW COOL

ADAPTED BY
JADE HEMSWORTH

BASED ON THE ORIGINAL SCREENPLAY BY
JORDANA ARKIN

[Imprint]
MAKE YOUR MARK

NEW YORK

[Imprint]
MAKE YOUR MARK

A part of Macmillan Children's Publishing Group

Project Mc². Copyright © 2016 by MGA, LLC. All rights reserved

Printed in the United States of America by R. R. Donnelley & Sons
Company, Harrisonburg, Virginia. For information, address
Imprint, 175 Fifth Avenue, New York, N.Y. 10010.

I.Y.C.Y.C.S.B.F.R.D.S.
(If You Care You Can Share But For Real Don't Steal.)

Library of Congress Cataloging-in-Publication Data is available.

ISBN 978-1-250-09890-0 (hardcover) /
ISBN 978-1-250-09892-4 (ebook)

Our books may be purchased in bulk for promotional, educational, or
business use. Please contact your local bookseller or the Macmillan
Corporate and Premium Sales Department at (800) 221-7945 ext. 5442
or by e-mail at MacmillanSpecialMarkets@macmillan.com.

KOOL-AID® is the registered trademark of
Kraft Food Group Brands, LLC

Imprint logo designed by Amanda Spielman

First Edition—2016

1   3   5   7   9   10   8   6   4   2

mackids.com

SPECIAL THANKS TO THOSE WHO ARE

I.A.A.A.T.S.T.*

Michael Anderson, Juli Boylan, Ruby Chang, Paula Garcia, Anne Gates, Leah George, Kris Marvin Hughes, Vicki Jaeger, Sam Khare, Katiedid Langrock, Claudia Leiva, Ilse Lopez, Corinne Mescher, Bruce Morrison, Sadaf Cohen Muncy, Dante Sandoval, Ellie Trope, Jeff Vinokur, and Isaac Larian.

*INTERESTING AND AMAZING AT THE SAME TIME

SMART IS THE NEW COOL

Prologue

She was still lost in a dream. McKeyla McAlister could hear the steady beeping of the alarm clock, persistent as it announced the day. She rolled over in bed and rubbed her eyes. The ceiling came into view above her, then the room, piled high with cardboard boxes containing everything she owned.

She sat up, reaching for the box labeled STUFF SO FRAGILE I WILL HURT SOMEONE IF IT BREAKS. Her composition notebook was perched right on top. She turned it over in her hands, thinking of the first day she'd opened this notebook—and how much it had guided her.

Lately, she felt like her life was filled with first days. The first day at a new school, the first day on her own, or the first day trying to fit in. She couldn't settle down anywhere long enough to have a favorite thrift store to shop at, or a sweet pug puppy, or a great bookstore to hang out in every weekend. She was kind of dreading spending another day in a classroom filled with strangers.

"Come on," she said, tucking the notebook under her arm. "Time to start the day."

She went to her closet, looking at the rack of clothes—denim jackets, sweaters, and flannel shirts all hung in a neat row. Right below them were several pairs of leather boots and sneakers. She ignored the clothes and pressed her hand against the small, flat screen on the wall next to the closet, letting the device scan her palm print. IDENTITY CONFIRMED.

The closet slid back into the wall, revealing a secret room. McKeyla slipped inside and the door closed behind her, hiding the room completely.

Time for her new mission to start.

Chapter One
I.A.W.A.T.S.T.*

Camryn Coyle leaned into a right turn, and Maywood Glen Academy appeared in front of her. Kids were crowded outside the massive stone school, sitting on the grass, sharing earbuds, or slurping down the last of their grande frappes and capps. She narrowed her beautiful brown eyes and leaned forward to pick up more speed as the road straightened out. Her skateboard could go twice as fast as others because she'd installed a sweet engine on the back. She'd even designed special goggles (complete with

*INTERESTING AND WEIRD AT THE SAME TIME

crack-proof lenses) and a matching indestructible helmet that fit over her long burgundy curls.

As she pulled up to the school, she stepped off the custom board and popped it into her arms. Despite the crowd, she instantly spotted her best friend, Bryden Bandweth, as usual completely absorbed in her phone. Bryden was a social media maven—if there was a social media platform worth anything, she was tapped into it. She had oodles of followers—and she followed ten times as many.

This morning, Bry, who had long, curly black hair and cocoa skin, couldn't be missed in an emoji T-shirt, a bright red skirt, and suspenders. When Cam caught up to her, they exchanged their signature greeting, a series of low fives and fist bumps in perfect sync.

While Cam was the most introverted of all her friends, Bryden was usually super peppy, talking twice as fast as everyone else and often going on long, rambling tangents sharing her every thought and feeling as soon as she had it. But today she seemed a little subdued, a little off. Slightly less . . . Bry.

"Sorry, Cam." She yawned. "I'm still in sleep mode. I was up sooooo late last night."

"Same," Cam commiserated. She could barely get out of bed this morning. She'd just thrown on her yellow print shorts and a floral baseball hat so she didn't have to worry about her hair. "I was practically comatose finishing this beast." Cam held up a thick stack of paper.

Bry's eyes went wide. "The *Macbeth* report! I totally spaced." She looked down at her cell, checking the minutes until the bell. "Oh good . . . still have time . . ."

She began furiously typing the paper on her cell phone. Bry was the absolute best at typing and talking at the same time. No one else could post a photo while carrying on two completely different, simultaneous conversations. Bry was also one of the friendliest girls at Maywood Glen Academy. She was friends with everybody.

"I was about to jam on it last night when this idea popped into my brain to take the camera chip out of one of my old cells and put it in my pen," Bry went on while also typing and walking.

"Like a selfie spy pen," Cam said.

"Exactly! I tried it out and spied on myself but pretended I didn't know I was spying on myself, so it was like I was spying on someone who wasn't me—but it really was me. I mean, the camera pen is cool and all, but I needed to write that report. There, *Macbeth* done! And I really gotta stop getting so distract—"

Before Bry could take a breath or finish her sentence, a tall, muscular boy with shaggy brown hair walked past them. She stopped in place, pointing her phone in his direction. "T.C.F.H.O.G."

"So true, Too Cute For His Own Good," Cam said, spelling out the acronym. Cam could speak Bryden, which meant she could easily decipher a series of complicated acronyms. They'd been communicating this way since they could spell. Sometimes Bry or Cam would ramble off a superlong one that no one else on earth would be able to get, but they knew each other so well that they always understood it.

As they walked up the steps and into the school, no one looked at them. The hall was strangely silent—almost every single person was watching something intensely on their phones.

"What's with all the cell zombies?" Cam asked, relatively curious.

"It's me! Stand back. . . . I'm trending." Bry was convinced it was her "yawnstagram," a picture she had snapped that morning of herself yawning, but as they peered over one girl's shoulder, Bry realized it was something else. Everyone was watching a video of a cute boy stepping out of a black sedan. He was wearing sunglasses and kept waving to the camera like he was a celebrity.

A reporter was speaking over the video. "Prince Xander, best known as the Thrillionaire Prince, is headed to the small U.S. town of Maywood Glen for his highly publicized trip to outer space, the latest of the popular British royal's international adventures."

Bry turned to Cam, her brown eyes bright and awestruck. "I can't believe he's coming *here* tomorrow!"

Cam smiled. "I can't believe tomorrow *is* tomorrow."

A few feet away, a group of girls were huddled in a circle, discussing the news. One wondered out loud if Prince Xander had a girlfriend—

she'd happily be his space princess—while the others were just dying to meet the handsome prince. They suddenly noticed Cam and Bry standing nearby, listening.

"Hey, Cam, doesn't your dad work at Space Inc.?" a wide-eyed girl asked.

"She could introduce us to the prince!" a girl wearing a polka-dotted dress added.

Within seconds, Cam was surrounded by the eager mob. Girls from all grades were asking her to get them passes for the launch or to sneak them into the prince's training facility.

"Sorry," Bry said, "but Cam would need top secret clearance from her dad, so . . . Forward slash, let's dash!" Bry pulled Cam away before the students smothered her.

Bry held on tight to Cam's hand as they raced down the hall, away from the growing crowd. They turned the corner, crashing into a girl in striped leggings and a leather jacket. Her books fell to the ground, just inches from her red plaid lace-up studded boots. Papers scattered all over the floor in a mess.

"I am soooo sorry!" Bry uttered, covering her hand with her mouth.

"Didn't mean to crash into you . . . " Cam apologized sincerely.

The girls knelt down, trying to gather the papers, composition notebook, and a folder with a photo of a boy with a huge grin sticking out the top. It took Bry a second to realize it was a pic of Prince Xander. Bry was a little confused and a lot intrigued, so she reached out to pick it up for the girl. "Let me help you with that. . . ."

"Thanks, I got her!" the girl said nervously, grabbing the notebook and papers before Bry could touch them. "I mean *it*. I got *it*."

"You're new, right?" Cam assumed. She hadn't seen her around Maywood Glen, and the town was small enough that she had met everyone *at least* once.

"Um, yes! I'm new, brand-new. That's what I am," the girl rambled nervously. "Just the new kid. No big deal." She had green eyes and long, wavy brown hair, which she tucked behind one ear. The girls waited for her to introduce herself, but she didn't.

"Great, so we just made a really bad impresh on the transfer student," Bry said.

She and Cam gave a mock cheer in unison.

"Go us!" They hoped a little humor might make the stranger more comfortable.

The mysterious girl just gave them a tight smile. "It's okay, really. No broken bones. No chipped teeth. No split ends. I'm fine, perfectly fine." She started to back away.

"I'm fine, too, McKeyla," blurted out a high-pitched girl's voice. Cam and Bry looked around for the speaker. Most of the hall was empty.

"Who said that?" Cam asked, confused.

"Said what?" The girl tried to brush off the question like it was no big deal. "I heard someone cough down the hall." She looked over Cam's and Bry's shoulders and called out, "You okay back there? I should go check."

"It wasn't a cough. . . . I heard *words*." Cam glanced sideways at Bry. With a glance back, Bry agreed that something was really strange about this girl. And where had that voice come from?

"It sounded like it came from your notebook. . . ." Bry pointed out.

"Oh, that? That was my cell." The girl pulled out her phone so quickly it was like a sleight-of-hand magic trick. She held it up to her ear and pretended to have a call. "What's up, girlfriend? Sure, let's meet at the mall . . . at some store . . . near some other store."

The girl pushed past them and hurried down the hallway, now chatting about the weather. Bry and Cam watched her go, squinting with suspicion.

"McKeyla, huh?" Bry said. "That girl is definitely I.A.W.A.T.S.T."

"Hmmm, Interesting And Weird At The Same Time," Cam agreed.

Cam and Bry went down the hall, chatting about the mystery girl. Why had she just transferred in now? Where did she buy those cute kicks?

But, more important, what was she hiding?

Chapter Two
N.G.O.T.S.*

Cam sat cross-legged on her bed, which was piled high with striped pillows and blankets for comfort. Her orange workbench ran the length of her room, with drills and saws and pliers hanging above it. When she was younger, while other little girls collected dolls and stuffed animals, Cam collected screwdrivers and drill bits. She spent practically every day after school working on new inventions, but today she and Bry were sprawled across the bed, just hanging out.

Cam was glued to her smartphone, checking

*NEW GIRL ON THE SCENE

out the latest post by Prince Xander, a video of himself talking about the space launch. He looked into the camera with his dreamy baby-blue eyes.

"I can't believe it! I'm finally taking the ultimate trip," he said, filming himself on his phone, selfie-style. His wavy brown hair spilled over his forehead. "As a kid I always wanted to go into space to fight aliens with laser swords, like in that documentary I saw about the war of the stars." He winked into the camera, and then the video cut out.

Cam couldn't help but smile. Yes, Prince Xander was the party-boy cousin of Britain's royal family. He'd been on the cover of every trashy tabloid in the world, but he was also kind of charming. And cute—definitely cute.

Meanwhile, Bry was lying on her stomach typing on her laptop. She had on her favorite pair of glasses—neon pixel-inspired frames—and they were practically fogging up from her getting more steamed with every keystroke. She made a frustrated noise and started banging her head on the keyboard. "Nothing! Nothing! Nothing!"

Cam grabbed Bry's shoulder, rescuing her friend. "Stop that! You're going to get keyboard forehead. *Again.* What's up?"

"So that girl at school, McKeyla? I found out that her last name is McAlister. I did a search on every social media site and can't find a single deet about who she is or where she's from." Bry sighed in exasperation.

"No way," Cam said, leaning over to look at the screen. "Nobody can hide from the Internet. Especially from *you.*"

"Except for *her.* . . . It's like she's some kind of ghost."

"Yeah, a very fashionable ghost," Cam agreed.

Suddenly, Cam heard footsteps on the stairs. She glanced out her bedroom door and saw her father, rubbing his temples as if he had a killer migraine.

"Dad?" Cam asked, surprised. "You're home early . . . ?" She left the *are you okay* part unspoken in the air.

Mr. Coyle hovered in Cam's doorway, offering the girls a tight smile. "Oh, there was just some commotion at the office today."

"Something's up at Space Inc.?" Cam asked. She rarely got worried, but something about her dad's face unsettled her. "What kind of commotion? What's wrong? What's going on?"

"Oh, how I love that excessively curious nature of yours," Mr. Coyle teased. It was true—Cam had always wanted to know how things worked and had been asking him questions ever since she could talk. She wanted to know everything about the work he did at Space Inc., about the planets and stars and Milky Way, about why a computer worked the way it did . . . and could she take it apart to see its hard drive?

"I got it from you," Cam shot back. Then she raised her brows as if to say *Okay . . . now, spill it.*

He didn't want his daughter to worry, but he knew that Cam was the inquisitive type who required an answer. "It's probably nothing," Mr. Coyle said, smoothing his hands on his brown cardigan while trying to convince himself that it was the truth. "We just received a strange phone call. Some type of threat against the prince's launch."

Cam shook her head. "Who would want to hurt the prince? He's harmless."

"And adorbs," Bry chimed in.

"And entertaining," Cam added.

"Which makes him totes adorbs!" Bry smiled.

"Um, I know, right? Totes adorbs." Mr. Coyle smiled awkwardly. Then he turned serious again and pulled out his phone. "Apparently *someone* doesn't agree with you."

He pressed PLAY on his screen, and an eerie, computerized voice filled the room.

"Attention, Space Inc: Dismantle your plans for the prince's launch immediately. I'm warning you—there will be devastating consequences if Prince Xander's flight is not canceled. That is all I can say."

Bry cringed. "Well, *I'm* totally creeped out."

Mr. Coyle just shrugged. "The office gets crazy messages like this all the time. Everyone thinks it's just another hoax."

"And you?" Cam said, looking at her father. He had that same tight look he always got when he was extra stressed.

"I'm . . ." He hesitated, glancing from Bry to Cam. "I'm not so sure. You see, last night I accidentally left my laptop at the office—closed—and this morning I found it open." He set his laptop bag on the bed next to them, as if presenting evidence.

"That's kinda freaky," Cam weighed in.

"I thought so, too!" Mr. Coyle said. "And with that weird phone call, I wonder if someone's after information about the flight."

Bry yanked out his laptop, cracked it open, and started clicking away. "If you want, Mr. Coyle, I can tap into Space Inc.'s security cams to see if someone has been lurking around there after hours. . . ."

Mr. Coyle let out a small laugh. "That's a nice offer, Bry, but it's impossible to break into our cameras. The firewall was specifically designed so that no one—"

"I'm in!" Bry said cheerfully, grinning at the screen.

Mr. Coyle, disturbed yet impressed, stepped forward, looking at the security footage from over her shoulder to see for himself. "Man . . . you are *really* good at this."

Bry hit the key that played the recorded black-and-white footage. There was an aerial shot of Mr. Coyle's desk with no one around. At the bottom of the frame was the time code. Bry fast-forwarded through the footage—until she saw a dark, shadowy figure enter the room. She instantly stopped it and let the footage play out. The person's face was obscured, covered by a hooded sweatshirt.

"Look! There!" Bry cried out. "Do you know who that is?"

Mr. Coyle squinted at the screen. The image was a little blurry. "I don't know. . . . It could be a janitor or a security guard."

Bry zoomed in on the image. "Looks like someone slender. . . ."

"Maybe the guard has been taking Pilates?" Mr. Coyle desperately joked.

"Is it a woman?" Bry asked.

Mr. Coyle shook his head in confusion as he looked intently at the screen for a second. Then he straightened up and put the laptop back in his bag. "I'd better go call security. . . . Thanks, girls," he added before rushing out the door.

Cam leaned in, whispering conspiratorially with her friend. "Now, think, Bry. Who in our tiny little town would want to threaten the prince and his mission?"

"Got me," Bry said, stumped. "It's the coolest thing to happen here since Emma Danielson thought that pop singer was following her 'grams and then found out it was a different girl with the same name."

Cam sparked with a wild idea. "Ahhh, but what if the blurry hacker isn't from *here*? What if it's someone who showed up out of nowhere, makes iffy excuses, and carts around a picture of the prince?"

Bry smiled and raised a brow, knowing exactly whom Cam meant. "Hmmmm . . . what an interesting and weird thought . . . at the same time."

"But how can we know for sure that it's McKeyla?"

Bry snapped her fingers. "What if we matched her fingerprints to the ones on your dad's laptop?"

"Very sly, Bry . . . If only we knew anything about lifting fingerprints."

Bry sat up and smirked "We don't. But we know someone who might. . . ."

Chapter Three
Y.C.C.I.R.A.T.*

Adrienne Attoms sat in the back of history class with perfect posture, watching interviews for the upcoming space launch on the television at the front of the room. Adrienne was the most girly of all her friends, with long blond hair and a fierce dedication to pastels. Her love of the pale colors was only trumped by her loves of pastry and the chemistry of baking it. She was wearing lavender and mint green. (Somehow it worked on her.)

The launch was taking place in less than thirty-two hours. A British reporter stood outside the

Space Inc. facility as Prince Xander was escorted in. The prince was flanked by bodyguards and his personal assistant, a thin brunette woman with sharp features.

"One-point-five million dollars," the reporter said. "An exorbitant amount of money by any account for a 'vacation.' But for Britain's own Prince Xander, it's another extreme stunt that has him, once again, in the international spotlight. Perhaps best put in his own noble words—"

"It's friggin' awesome!" the prince shouted out as he waved to the massive crowd outside the gates. They cheered him on, and he ate it up.

Adrienne wasn't studying the screen, though—her intense focus was trained on a girl with long, wavy brown hair. McKeyla, or "M" as she had told their teacher she preferred to be called, sat in the front row staring up at the TV. She was absently twirling a pen in her fingers.

"I'm so happy you're helping us," Cam whispered from behind her.

"Anytime," Adrienne, or Adri, as her friends called her, said in her distinctive Spanish accent.

Cam and Bry had approached her that morning, asking if she wanted to be part of a "top secret investigation." Adri was the best and youngest culinary chemist in the entire United States. When anyone wondered out loud if *culinary chemist* was really a thing, Adri would emphatically say, "Yes, it's a thing!"). See, she was born and raised in Spain, where she learned culinary chemistry from her grandmother, her *abuela*, who taught her how to make drinks that tasted like cookie dough and gum that bubbled up in your mouth the more it was chewed.

But today Adri had something else brewing: helping Cam and Bry get and verify fingerprints from McKeyla McAlister, the girl they suspected of sabotaging the prince's launch. Not an easy task, but there were three of them and only one of her. The odds were in their favor.

After studying McKeyla's every move, Adri turned to her friends. "Now is our chance." She stood up and strutted to the front of the room. But when she passed McKeyla, she flung her body forward, quite dramatically, pretending she'd tripped on one of McKeyla's purple boots.

"Oh no!" Adri said, looking up at her target. She started talking with her hands, trying to distract her. She was by far the most dramatic of all three girls . . . and a little goofy, too. "I'm so sorry! I didn't see your petite little feet there! By the way, nice boots. We haven't met. I'm Adrienne Attoms. Adri. Wanna do lunch sometime? I am such a foodie. I know all the fanciest places to eat in this town. There's, like, two. But they're fabulous!"

Before McKeyla could respond, Adri moved her hand in a great sweeping arc, sending M's pen flying to the back of the room. It landed right at Cam's and Bry's feet, and Bry quickly snatched it up—holding it carefully by one end so she didn't smudge any fingerprints.

McKeyla jumped up and walked to the back, scanning the floor for her missing pen. It was obviously in Bry's hand. M looked somewhat embarrassed as she said, "Hey, you guys again. I can't seem to hang on to my supplies around you. Weird, huh? That's my pen . . . ?"

"You don't want this pen," Bry said, starting into one of her rambles. "It got sticky. From the sticky ground. But I like sticky things . . . sticky notes, sticky glue, sticky rice, sticky tape. . . . So here, take mine!"

Bry handed her a pen sitting on her desk. M narrowed her eyes, unsure if something peculiar was going on, but she took it anyway. "Um . . . thanks . . ." she said, then walked away.

Bry, Adri, and Cam all stared at M's pen, which was now sitting on Bry's desk. They had finally got their first piece of evidence! High fives all around!

❦ ❦ ❦

Adri darted excitedly around her kitchen, a measuring cup in each hand. She had on her favorite apron, the one with little cupcakes all over it that she wore whenever she was working on a special recipe. The counter was covered with the necessary supplies: clear tape, cinnamon and sugar, black construction paper, Mr. Coyle's laptop, and McKeyla's pen.

As Bry and Cam stood at the ready, Adri took command of the kitchen, narrating each step, as she always did. It was almost like she was starring in her own cooking show. "You pour in a quarter cup of flour and two dashes of cinnamon. Dash! Dash! Then mix it up." She stirred the ingredients together in the bowl, waiting until it was a uniform color. She reached out her hand to Bry. "And now . . . the pen . . ."

Bry cautiously removed M's pen from a plastic bag with tongs so she wouldn't ruin the prints. She passed it to Adri, who carefully took it by each end.

"Roll it, dust it . . . take the tape and press down lightly. Pat! Pat! Pat!" Adri sang out as she rolled the pen in the mixture, then brushed the extra powder off with a pastry brush, took a piece of clear tape, and pressed it to the side of the pen, right where the biggest print would be. "And *olé*! The print!"

"Rad!" Cam said, staring at the print on the tape. "Homemade fingerprint kit."

"*And* it's great for churros!" Adri laughed as she took a tray of churros out of the oven and rolled them in the remaining mixture, plus sugar, of course.

Bry aimed her cell phone at the fingerprint, capturing a picture. She opened a code scanner app of her own design and uploaded the print. "Hey, we did it. We got a partial print. . . ."

Cam swiftly brushed the last of Adri's mixture onto her dad's laptop cover, then lifted the print using the clear tape. She immediately handed the piece to Bry to scan. When Bry uploaded that print into the app, her phone beeped.

"And a partial match!" Bry said, smiling. "Go, us! Now we know for sure that McKeyla's the bad guy . . . or girl."

Adri furrowed her brows. "I don't know. If this girl is really involved in something as huge as threatening the prince's flight, I think we'll need more proof than a partial print, even one that tastes as good as it looks."

Bry stared at the phone screen and that definitive word: MATCH. How could it not be enough proof? The word *match* was in all caps.

"We could tell your dad," Adri suggested to Cam.

"Sure, *he'll* believe us," Cam said, her mouth full of a piping-hot churro. "But who's going to believe *him*? Adri's right, Bry. We need more evidence."

Needing to think this through, Bry set down her phone and put her chin in her hands. "Well, then I guess we'll just have to catch this McKeyla McAlister in the act of doing something worth catching!"

Chapter Four
I.S.O.O.T.G.G.I.M.G.*

McKeyla walked home from school with her backpack on one shoulder and the composition notebook tucked under her arm. She was the epitome of cool in her slouchy purple hat, long burgundy sweater, and up-cycled tee. The earbuds plugged into her ears ensured that she didn't hear the three girls following her.

Adri, Cam, and Bry were dashing from tree to tree. They squeezed themselves behind one trunk, peered out across the sidewalk, then ducked behind some shrubbery. When M

*IS SHE ONE OF THE GOOD GUYS . . . I MEAN GIRLS?

hooked a left, a right, and another left, then went inside her plain, unassuming tan house, the girls ran around the side.

"Go, go, go, go," Bry whispered, ushering the girls toward the backyard. There wasn't much there—no patio furniture or barbecue grill, unlike in most normal yards. It looked as if no one lived in the house. They plopped down in the bushes, staring at an open window on the side of the house. McKeyla appeared for a few seconds, then pulled the curtains closed. They groaned.

"Now what do we do?" Adri fretted. "We can't see or hear what she's doing in there."

Cam riffled through her backpack. She pulled out one of her favorite inventions for eavesdropping. She'd spent three whole weeks working on it, trying to get it just right. Her dad had grounded her for breaking curfew and she'd wanted to know (1) if she'd ever be un-grounded, and (2) what she was getting for Christmas. Plus, her new next-door neighbor was pretty cute. It wouldn't hurt to know if he was crushing on her like she was crushing on him. (Verdict: He was!)

The clear plastic bowl-shaped object was attached to a small, battery-powered speaker. She held them both in the air, and it transmitted sounds from inside the house. They could clearly hear McKeyla, and she was most definitely up to something. They huddled closer to listen.

"Give me a sec, Addison," M's voice said. "I want to check the news before reporting back to headquarters."

"Sweet," Adri said, adjusting her chic lavender glasses. "But I wish we could get a peek inside and see what she's doing."

"Camera pen!" Bry smirked as she hit a button on her smartphone, syncing it with the camera pen. Within seconds, the three girls had a view of McKeyla's room. The image kept jumping around because McKeyla was walking around with the pen, but they were still able to catch glimpses of her box-filled room and cluttered desk.

"The Quail wants to brief you on the mission status right now," a somewhat-familiar voice said offscreen.

"The Quail?" Cam whispered. "That must

be a code name for the evil mastermind she's working for!"

On-screen, McKeyla approached her walk-in closet, pressing her hand to an electronic scanning device that recognized her handprint and granted her access. The door slid back, revealing a secret laboratory. Beakers filled with colorful liquids were scattered on countertops, and there were several computers with different data on each screen. A red lava light with floating blobs sat next to an open laptop.

"Who the heck *is* this girl?" Cam said to the girls while staring at the live feed.

"Who wants to know?" said McKeyla as the camera view flipped around to her face.

Busted! Cam, Adri, and Bry squealed and scrambled to their feet, trying to gather all their stuff and take off, but McKeyla made it outside in a flash to confront them. "So . . . you were all spying on me?" she accused.

"Please don't hurt us," Bry begged, her words running into one another. "We were just . . ."

"We were just . . ." Cam added, trying to help Bry explain.

Adri gave it a shot: "We were just . . . uh . . ."

"Spying on me," M repeated. "Isn't that right, Adrienne Attoms? Or was this your idea, Bryden Bandweth? Or yours, Camryn Coyle?"

"She. Knows. Us," Bry whispered.

"Of course I do," M said. "My organization researches all my new schools before I arrive. They said you're the three smartest girls at Maywood Glen Academy."

"Not surprised," Adri said, tossing her ponytail over her shoulder proudly.

"I'm surprised," a voice sniped.

"Is that a talking notebook?" Adri stared at the composition notebook tucked under McKeyla's arm. Her hand drifted toward McKeyla as if to grab it, and M possessively clutched it tighter and twisted away.

Cam pointed at it. "I *knew* it!"

"I'm not an *it*!" the voice said indignantly. "My name is A.D.I.S.N. Pronounced 'Addison.' Short for 'Advanced Digital Intelligence Spy Notebook.' Heavy on the intelligence. Unlike others out here! *Hmmph!*"

"A.D.I.S.N., quiet!" McKeyla said quickly,

and refocused on the girls. "Let's hope you know enough not to tell anyone what you saw here today," she said sternly.

Bry's heart was racing. What exactly *had* they seen? She swallowed hard. "We won't . . . but please don't hurt us!"

"Relax, I'm one of the good guys. . . . I mean, *girls*," M said.

"OMG, she's not going to kill us!" Bry laughed, relieved.

"So why are you here, in our town, at our school?" Cam asked curiously.

"I'm here on a highly classified mission. That's all I can say." She stared at Cam's plastic contraption, then pointed at it. "Cool listening device . . . Did you make that?"

"Yeah, thanks!" Cam smiled. "I call it my . . . Sound Catcher." Catching the mystified looks of the other girls, she added, "I'm great at making things, bad at naming them."

"Nice work," McKeyla said. "I'm McKeyla McAlister."

Bry started thinking about M's name . . . *really* thinking about it. "Whoa, whoa . . .

McKeyla McAlister. That's M-c . . . M-c-squared! No way. I'm squared, too—B-squared. Cam is C-squared and Adri is A-squared."

"We're, like, a supercute, live version of the Pythagorean theorem," Cam grinned.

M tilted her head to the side, considering it. "Well, I can honestly say I've never met a human equation before."

"Listen, M," Cam said, peering around her at the open window. "We promise not to say a word . . . if you let us check out that awesome stuff you have in there. I've got total lab envy."

Bry took a step forward, inching toward the window. M moved aside to block her. "Okay, look, I can see you guys are pretty into gadgets and high-tech stuff, but unfortunately I can't let you—"

Seeing her chance, Cam slipped around the other side of M and jumped up to climb through the window. Bry and Adri followed close behind.

"Wait! Stop!" M called out, knowing it was too late.

The girls were already inside the house. When they got a full look at the lab, it was even more impressive than at first glance. It was like a superspy science playground! There were half-constructed experiments, holographic maps, and state-of-the-art computer equipment. A long desk had a massive flat-screen TV above it. On a worktable filled with circuit boards, tools, and wires, Cam discovered a small recycled robot M had been working on. M tried to stop her from touching it, but Cam inserted a soda can into the base, which made the robot start walking.

"It works?" M exclaimed. She had been having trouble figuring out how to complete the mechanism.

Cam shrugged matter-of-factly. "All it needed was a cylindrical base."

Meanwhile, Bry was poking at a holographic projector showing the planets in the solar system, and Adri was having a blast creating smoke screens by combining different chemicals from a bunch of beakers and an amazing chemistry kit that folded up into its own red case.

Finally, M couldn't take everyone messing with her experiments anymore.

"Okay, that's it. Time to go!" she cried while

attempting to usher the over-excited and definitely over-interested girls out of her private space. She'd always worked alone. She'd spent afternoons investigating—alone. And eating lunch—alone. And watching television—alone. She'd never needed any company before, and she wasn't about to change that now.

She pointed to the door, but the girls didn't seem to notice her. Adri was already mixing another batch of chemicals in a smoking test tube, and Bry was leaning over M's keyboard, feverishly typing. A.D.I.S.N. started repeating "Incoming transmission!" and, suddenly, the large TV monitor over the desk turned on. A striking, sophisticated older woman with sleek black hair and serious eyes stared down at them.

"Agent McAlister. You have friends in your *private* lab?" the woman asked in an accusatory tone. She looked a bit like M, with high cheekbones and fair skin.

McKeyla stood up straight, obviously intimidated. "Yes, ma'am. I mean, no, ma'am. Somehow, these girls followed me home, and then they jumped through the window before I could—"

"I see," the woman said, cutting her off. "Well,

then I should say hello to Adrienne, Bryden, and Camryn."

The girls' mouths dropped. *She. Knows. Us. Too?*

"I'm the Quail," the woman said, introducing herself. "And a member of NOV8—that's 'innovate'—an elite organization of women operatives from all over the globe. Yes, it's true—women *do* run the world. We make it a point to be aware of exceptionally intelligent females. Top students, like you girls, are always on our radar."

Bry turned to her friends. "So we're on the radar of a real, live top secret organization with a crazy-cool code name? Hashtag amazeblogs!"

"I can't believe this!" Cam said, euphoric. She was usually the calmest of the group, but even she was bouncing on her toes, mimicking her friend Bry.

"So . . . is M here 'cause of the threats made on the prince's mission?" Bry asked, talking so fast she could barely keep up with herself. "And if so, is that why she was hacking Mr. Coyle's laptop? And who do you think wants to stop the launch? And why? And when? And how? And you should know that once I start asking

questions it's hard for me to stop unless someone answers me."

The Quail furrowed her brow. "You're aware
of Agent McAlister accessing the laptop?"

"My dad works at Space Inc.," Cam explained.

"And we did some investigating of our own,
like swapping out M's pen for a homemade video-
monitoring device," Bry said, waving the camera
pen in the air.

McKeyla looked embarrassed. "I never had
any reason to suspect it was a camera pen," she
explained sheepishly.

"And I used an old family recipe to get her
fingerprints off her pen," Adri disclosed.

The Quail nodded, taking it all in. "Since you
already know more than you should, I will tell
you that once NOV8 received inside intel that the
prince's mission may be in danger, we sent Agent
McAlister to Maywood Glen to find out whatever
she could first and then protect the prince once
he arrived." She fixed Cam, Bry, and Adri in her
gaze. "I must say, I'm rather impressed with your
keen instincts and experimental methods. NOV8
needs new recruits. If you're interested, I'd like to

test you out in the field under the leadership of Agent McAlister."

M's jaw dropped. "With all due respect"— she nervously rocked back on her heels— "there's an extremely tight deadline. We have just twenty-three hours until the launch, then I leave immediately, so I don't think—"

"I know you'll do an impeccable job guiding these girls on this time-sensitive assignment before your next mission," the Quail interrupted.

M tried to turn her face into something normal. Was she rolling her eyes? She was probably rolling her eyes.

It was just that she'd *always* worked on her own. McKeyla McAlister: smart, tough, and (most important!) independent. That was what she was known for. Now the Quail wanted her to have three trainees following her around like over-excited puppies? How exactly was that going to work?

M looked up at the Quail, waiting for her to realize this was terrible idea, but the Quail didn't say anything. She just smiled.

"Of course, ma'am . . ." M finally agreed.

With that, the screen went black. Adri, Bry, and Cam let out squeals of delight while throwing their arms around one another for a victorious group hug. Bry was jumping up and down on her toes so much the liquid in the beakers sloshed back and forth.

When they threw their arms around M to include her in the celebration, McKeyla kept her hands stiffly at her side, unprepared to hug them back. She was used to working alone. In fact, she was not into taking risks involving other people. When she'd teamed up before, it had led to disaster.

What would happen this time?

Chapter Five
T.S.P.O.S.A.*

The next morning, McKeyla leaned back in her desk chair, munching on her first bowl of cereal for the day. She'd hoped to wake up energized and ready to tackle the mission in front of her. But instead she was filled with dread. Just eleven hours until the launch, and she had three new recruits to train, unless she could convince her boss that she was better off working solo.

This wasn't going to be good. . . .

"Is this really the time to be taking chances?" M asked, pushing herself around the lab in her chair. She looked up at the screen, studying the Quail's expression. "The prince is unpredictable enough on his own."

*THE SECRET PART OF SECRET AGENT

"Yes, and the threat to his mission is very real," the Quail said. "Since we have yet to verify its source, NOV8 wants you to have the extra support. Is that understood, Agent McAlister?"

M let out a deep sigh. "Understood . . ."

"Good." The Quail smiled and her tone softened. "Now, remember to call Grandma. It's her birthday."

"Don't worry, Mom. I didn't forget."

"Love you, sweetheart."

"Love you, too." M closed the video chat, annoyed with herself that she couldn't persuade her mom to let her do the mission by herself. She didn't want to work with Adri, Bry, and Cam, but she had no other choice.

"Ugh," A.D.I.S.N. said from her station on the desk. Whenever she wanted to talk to McKeyla, her front cover glowed. If it was safe, M would open the book and speak directly to the screen displaying A.D.I.S.N.'s face—an emoji with a brown ponytail and glasses. "So much for getting out of working with those clingy troublemakers. I mean, as your bestie, and link to NOV8, I support you one hundred percent."

McKeyla smiled. For a secret agent's

computer sidekick, A.D.I.S.N. certainly had her own opinions.

"Who knows?" M said. "Maybe they'll pleasantly surprise us."

Just then, the doorbell rang. McKeyla went to the foyer and was surprised to be greeted by three girls in over-the-top spy costumes. Cam was dressed like Sherlock Holmes, while Adri and Bry looked more like modern James Bonds (if James Bond were a teenage girl with long, flowing hair and the right shade of lipstick). Adri held out a plate of treats and said, "One smart cookie? Before we go protect the prince and save the world from evildoers?"

"I like that you're all so . . . *enthusiastic*," M started, quickly stifling a laugh. "But before we go anywhere, I'd like to get a sense of your skills. Consider it an ops test."

"Sounds official," Cam said eagerly.

"Just point me toward your supplies and I'll whip something up!" Adri offered.

Within minutes, they were in M's lab. Adri was hunched over a row of beakers and ingredients, while Cam tinkered with a pile of wires and batteries M had lying around. Bry was hacking into social media sites on M's computer.

An hour later, M visited Adri, who'd baked a giant volcano cake, which she'd covered with gooey chocolate frosting.

"Sweet volcano cake," M said. "But how exactly will this help us protect the prince?"

"Well," Adri said, raising her eyebrows meaningfully, "what if there's a special occasion that calls for . . . an explosive distraction?" She poured a cup of liquid into the volcano, and thick pink foam exploded from the top!

"Promising." McKeyla nodded . . . and then she looked down.

"Oops, got some lava on your cute kicks!" cried Adri.

"And it's oozing into my socks," M said with some annoyance.

Before she could go clean off her boots, Bry held a phone in M's face, snapping a picture. "Ops test, my turn. Smile!"

Bry hit a few buttons on her screen, and M's picture appeared on every computer and tablet in the room. M panicked and ran from one to the next, trying to power down the screens or cover them.

"While I appreciate your tech aptitude, I can't afford to be on every social media site in the universe," M said. "Maybe you're not getting the *secret* part of *secret agent*?"

"Exhale," Bry said, holding up her hand. "I just hacked into your lab's wireless system and posted it to the IP addresses on the devices in this room. Only we can see it." Bry tapped something into her phone, and all the pictures of M disappeared. "There! Insta-gone!"

"Thank you." M breathed a sigh of relief. She heard a noise and turned, catching Cam as she drilled the last screw into a board with wires coming out of it. She had headphones on, but the music was blasting so loud the rest of them could hear it. She looked like she was heading to a party in her sparkly skull tank top and pink head kerchief, instead of engineering some serious equipment. "So your special skill is torturing the enemy by bursting their eardrums?" McKeyla asked, baffled.

Cam kept her head down, bobbing in time with the beat. It took her a second to notice M was looking right at her. "Hey, I'm finished!" she said.

"What is it?"

"Well, it *was* a bunch of useless parts," Cam said, "but now it's a portable police scanner with added features. I call it . . . Cam's Portable Police Scanner with Added Features. Remember, good with gadgets, not at naming them."

M put the headphones on. With a flip of a switch, the music changed to the police's radio frequency. M went through a few different channels, listening to conversations about neighborly disputes, cats that had gotten stuck in trees, and neighbors arguing about how the cats kept getting stuck in their trees.

"This can help us locate the prince through the security detail they're planning for him," McKeyla said, smiling at Cam, amazed. "Nice work!"

Cam stood there, waiting for M to go on, but she didn't. Bry and Adri were right behind her. "So . . ." Cam started to ask for all of them. "Did we pass the ops test?"

McKeyla was still studying the handmade scanner. She nodded as she turned the knob to a different channel. Bry jumped up and down on her toes. She'd worn her luckiest shirt today— a neon tank with white stars—and she knew it had done the trick. "Yay! Go, us!"

Bry and Cam broke into a familiar dance, hip-bumping and waving their hands in the air in unison. "*We passed, uh-huh,*" they sang. "*We passed... Oh yeah...*"

"*Me too,*" Adri added, dancing along with them, even though it was hard in her Mary Jane heels. "*With you... Me too...*"

M ignored them as she turned the dial and found a station where police officers were talking about the prince's movements around the city. Dozens of Maywood Glen police were looped in on his comings and goings, and they were discussing his transportation to the launch.

"He's heading toward Reardon Road," a man's voice said over the headphones. "We should be at the space station facility in a half hour or so."

M grabbed a notepad, furiously jotting down the details of the route. When she was done, she looked at her trio of trainees and grinned. Maybe her mom *was* right—maybe they *could* be helpful on this assignment.

Or at least not totally mess it up.

Chapter Six
A.D.W.P.C.*

Adri peered through NOV8's signature spy glasses, taking in the scene outside the space training facility. There was a security booth, one guard at the main gate, and a high wrought-iron fence that ran along the perimeter. There was no easy way to get inside and reach the prince.

She scanned the rest of the property, stopping at a black car parked near the main building. "Oooohhh, do you see that car?" she asked. "Looks *muy* suspicious to me."

Cam took the glasses. "Hmmm . . . tinted windows. No license plate. Sketch."

Bry agreed, "Super sketch."

She passed the binoculars to M, who zoomed in on the emblem on the front of the car. It had a strange star logo on the hood. "That's got to be them. Whoever wants to stop the prince, they're moving in fast," M said. "We have to get past that guard and get to the prince before they do."

"I got this covered," Bry said confidently as she typed something into her phone. Within seconds, the guard at the front gate heard a sound, walked into the booth, and started watching something on his computer screen that made him laugh like a little kid.

"Amazing." M smiled. "What'd you do?"

"I just rerouted his computer to stream an endless loop of funny cat videos," Bry said. "He should be distracted for at least an hour."

"Impressive," admitted M.

"Now, let's hurry before he catches on. . . ." Cam started toward the front gate, waving for the others to follow. She'd brought her skateboard, strapped over her backpack, knowing it could help if they needed to make a fast getaway.

The girls scurried past the security booth, ducking below the window so the guard wouldn't see. Not that anything would distract him from the brave kitten meeting a dog for the first time.

Adri, Bry, and Cam tiptoed exaggeratedly next to M, trying to be as sneaky as possible. Instead, they looked like they were bouncing.

"Since NOV8 wants me to guide you," McKeyla said, "here's lesson number one: Secret agents don't bounce."

"Oopsies!" Adri whispered.

"And they don't say 'oopsies,'" McKeyla added.

M maneuvered down a long corridor, finally spotting an open hangar they'd seen the prince go into an hour before. She imagined it was where he was preparing for the launch. There was only one problem: Stationed outside the hangar were three guards and a man in a black suit—the same man who'd stood near the prince in all his interviews.

"Hey, hey, hey, where do you girls think you're going?" the man in the black suit asked in a thick British accent. "And how did you get in here?" *This must be the prince's bodyguard,* M thought. "There are no visitors inside. You lot will have to go home and swoon over the prince's Snapbook, like all the other fangirls."

"Uhhhh . . . you're mixing up your social media," Bry said in her classic zippy tone. She wanted to help this man, who, obviously, wasn't social media savvy.

"Sir, you don't understand," M started, lifting the brim of her fedora so he could see her face. "I work for an elite organization of woman operatives from all over the world—"

The guards grabbed each of the girls by the arm and started escorting them away.

Cam looked to M, panicked. "Is this what normally happens?"

"No. Not when I'm on my own," McKeyla grumbled.

"What do we do now?" Adri asked.

M kept walking with the guard, pretending to leave, silently noting a fire alarm box on a pole as they walked past. She waited a beat and then said, "*This* is what I call a red alert." She stopped suddenly, twisting both arms free from the guard's grasp, and ran for the fire alarm. The other girls watched in awe as McKeyla executed a totally fierce high kick, aiming her red boot perfectly at the glass covering the box and smashing it open. It set off a loud, screeching alarm and startled the guards.

The other girls acted fast. Bry pulled out her cell phone, aiming it right in one guard's eyes. "Say cheese!" She clicked the turbo flash setting, then snapped a photo, momentarily blinding him. It was just the chance she needed to break free.

Cam twisted out of the guard's grip, but there were two of them blocking her and Adri's path. She whipped her skateboard from her back and set it on the ground. In one swift motion, she hurled it toward their feet, knocking the guards off balance. Then Adri and Cam darted down the corridor after M and Bry.

But Adri, trying hard to keep up in her dainty Mary Jane pumps, was going half as fast as Cam.

"Next time we try to save the world," Cam said, "wear flats!"

"I would never!" Adri said in her lilting Spanish accent.

The four girls ran toward Prince Xander's

bodyguard. He darted in front of the hangar, try-ing to block them. Adri stomped her heel into the center of his foot, causing him to hunch over in pain. She sniffed in satisfaction, threw her purse over her shoulder, and teetered quickly after the others as they raced inside the hangar.

"L.C.T.O.F.A.C.," yelled Bry.

"Yeah, Let's Call That Our Flash And Crash!" cheered Cam.

Prince Xander was standing in front of a table of flight equipment. He was wearing the Space Inc. uniform, a blue jumpsuit with black stripes at the shoulders. Bry, Cam, and Adri stared, their mouths agape. They were in the same space as a real, live prince, breathing the same royal air!

McKeyla knew she had to be precise and quick with His Royal Highness. "Prince Xander, we're here because—"

"My apologies, sir," his bodyguard said, rush-ing in behind the girls with the other guards. They started to pull the girls away.

"Wait, wait, gents," Prince Xander said, smil-ing. "I'd like to know just what this pretty lady thinks is so important that she had to interrupt my final training session before I leave the planet." He gestured at his assistant. "Jillian, my mouthwash."

Without waiting for a reply, he walked toward M, taking her hand in his own. She immediately slid her fingers out from underneath his. The prince might have a pleasant face, but his head was bigger than Mars. She could never be interested in someone so shallow and obsessed with himself.

"Prince, sir," M started, "I'm afraid your life is in danger. I'm a highly trained operative sent to protect you until you are safely on that capsule."

"Now, that's a good one!" The prince laughed, exposing his pearly-white, perfectly straight teeth. "You fangirls come up with the craziest stories just to get an autograph. Jillian, a pen!"

His assistant, a tiny, bird-faced woman with her hair pulled into a bun, fumbled around in her purse. Prince Xander waited all of a second, then strode over to a scientist in a lab coat and yanked a pen from his pocket.

"Oh no . . ." M clarified to the pompous prince. "I'm *not* a fan."

"Not a fan? Not a follower? But you are a girl! After I sign this for you," the prince went on, "you all have to go. It's not fair if you get to stay while the rest of my followers have to wait for the launch tonight."

Bry jumped forward, hoping to connect with him and become fast friends. "Hi, I'm Bry—well, Bryden is my full name. Bandweth. That's my last name. Bryden Bandweth. I'm an operative, too. Well, operative-in-training."

Bry curtsied, then turned to her friends. "I just rambled in front of a prince," she whispered, her words running into each other. "Hashtag I rule!"

The prince furrowed his brows. "Operatives, you say?"

"Yes! We work for this amazing organization of incredibly smart women," Adri said, tossing her blond hair over her shoulder with an exaggerated flair.

"Actually, *I* work for them, and the three of them are just helping out—though not so much at the moment," M said to stop the fangirling. She turned back to the prince. "Prince Xander, we have strong reason to believe there's a plot in action at this very moment. People out there could be trying to kidnap you."

"People want to kidnap me?" the prince asked with feigned shock. "Of course they do! Look at me!"

"I see that," Adri said, peering over her glasses.

"Look," M went on, "it's my job to keep anything bad from happening to you."

"Well, you're wasting your time with me," Prince Xander said. He jumped up onto an elevated platform, striding along fearlessly, as if he weren't five feet off the ground. "I'm famous and I like to speak my mind. If I had a pound for every threat made against my life, I could take all of you to space with me."

"Are you serious?" Cam asked excitedly. "I could hitch a ride on a fully orbital commercial spacecraft?"

Prince Xander frowned as if to say *I was obviously kidding*. Cam visibly deflated. "Right. You were just making a point."

"All I need is for you to stay alive long enough

to get on that flight," M said. "So please, let me just take you somewhere safer than this."

"That's what this is all about?" the prince asked, combing his fingers through his wavy brown hair. "I was planning on spending the afternoon in my hotel suite, but I guess I could spend it with four sharp, cute girls instead. Jillian, my things."

He jumped down from the platform as his assistant, Jillian, frantically pulled things together. His bodyguard stepped forward in an effort to derail this potential train wreck. "Sir— it'll be a clearance nightmare to transport you."

Jillian nodded her head, totally agreeing with him. "Yes, Your Highness. With the launch tonight, I really don't think you should—"

"Go in my spacesuit?" he asked while unzipping, revealing his white tank top and jeans. "I agree. Now, what are we waiting for? Ring my driver. Gather my luggage. We're going to party, Maywood Glen–style!" The bodyguard and Jillian followed, exceptionally displeased.

Adri, Bry, and Cam quickly followed them out the door, unable to believe their luck. Prince

Xander was goofy, fun, and totally adorbs. Was this British prince really going to hang out with them all afternoon?

We got him to hang with us. Now we get down to work, thought M. It was their responsibility to keep him safe until he made it onto the spacecraft. She'd have to watch out for that black car, and whoever made the threat against the prince, and try to figure out why they'd made it, and then anticipate what would come next, all while monitoring three new recruits who weren't adequately trained in the field.

So basically she'd have to do everything.

No pressure, right?

Chapter Seven
T.N.S.S.H.*

Prince Xander took a slow lap around Bryden's living room, drinking in the ceramic plate collectibles and the cozy family photos sitting above the entertainment center. There was a bowl of fruit on the coffee table, a few hand-painted vases Bryden's mom had made, and Mr. Bandweth's favorite green armchair, which no one else was allowed to sit in. The prince immediately sat in it.

"Not exactly the local hot spot I was expecting . . ." he murmured regretfully.

"Oh, gee, sorry there aren't velvet footstools and funny court jesters to entertain you," M said snidely. Just then, Jillian walked in carrying one of the prince's travel footstools—he liked her to bring it wherever he went. "Okay, I was half wrong."

McKeyla knew the prince wanted them to take him to some fancy club or sleek lounge, but they couldn't risk being in public with only six hours until the launch. Bryden's house was on the way to the launch site, her parents weren't home, and no one would expect to find a prince there. It was as safe as an unofficial safe house could get.

"Now, if you'll excuse me," M said, pulling out her notebook, "I have life-and-death matters to tend to. Meaning *your* life."

"Right, got that." The prince smirked, as if he didn't quite believe her.

Bry took a deep breath and stepped forward, still a little starstruck. "Hiiiii. This is my house. Bryden Bandweth. We met back at the training facility a while back? You remember, right? Or maybe not. I don't know. And now I'm just wasting what little time you have left here. If only I could control-alt-delete . . ." she said under her breath as she turned away in embarrassment.

"Nice to meet you. I'm Adrienne Attoms!" Adri said, stepping toward the prince. "Growing up in Spain, I traveled to London all the time. I love everything British except the food. Terribly bland! Bleh!"

"Rubbish," he protested.

"Exactly! It *does* taste like garbage!"

"Who cares about food?" Cam interjected. "We should be discussing the spacecraft's thrust-to-weight ratio! Happen to know what that is?"

The prince just shrugged. "All I know is that they're going to blast me into the sky"—he made rocket sounds while shooting his hand like it was a spaceship blasting off—"where I'll film my most epic online video. Then they'll bring me back down to Earth."

"Bringing you back down to Earth would be a *good* thing," M muttered under her breath. Then she glanced up, realizing everyone had heard that and was now staring at her. "Uh, I mean, 'cause everyone will miss you so much down here!" she said, faking enthusiasm.

The prince just ignored her. "Isn't there

anything fun to do around here?" he said, glancing around the humdrum room.

Bry lit up with a fresh idea. "Ever see someone play bananas like a piano?" Bry asked, her voice bubbly.

The prince looked confused. Bry grabbed three bananas out of the fruit bowl and brought them over to her soundboard on the table. "You never know when you need to hook something up. Like now." Bry quickly wired up the bananas so that every time you touched one, a different note sounded. She'd learned to play everything from "Heart and Soul" to "Chopsticks"—well, that was pretty much the playlist: "Heart and Soul" and "Chopsticks."

"Musical bananas, this is genius," cried the prince, delighted by the distraction.

Bry beamed, so pleased that the prince liked it.

M turned to her notebook. She asked A.D.I.S.N. to collect more data about the launch. "NOV8 has uncovered information regarding the prince's flight trajectory," A.D.I.S.N. said, then asked suspiciously, "Hey, what's that noise? Are you having a party? You didn't invite me?"

"It's not a party, A.D.I.S.N. It's a banana piano lesson," M reassured her. It was kind of crazy. Sometimes A.D.I.S.N. acted like a real, jealous friend. (Honestly, her *only* friend—it was hard to make friends when she moved after every mission.) A.D.I.S.N. got upset if McKeyla didn't bring her everywhere she went, and she was constantly reminding her that the new recruits were just that—recruits, not new friends.

"Ohhh," A.D.I.S.N. said, relieved that there were only a few people there. "Our complete projection of the spaceflight index shows that, at its peak, the prince's capsule will come in close proximity to a U.S. government cybersecurity satellite."

"A government satellite?" M asked, a bit baffled. "What could that have to do with the threats?"

A.D.I.S.N. started to reply, but the noise level in the room drowned her out. The prince was jamming on the banana keyboard, rocking out to an improvised song.

"Bravo, bravo!" M said sarcastically. "Now, can you please play a quieter fruit? We're running out of time and I really need to concentrate."

Prince Xander flashed a mischievous smile. M thought he looked like a bratty little kid in his red-and-white-striped shirt, which he'd paired with a shirt with motorcycles on it. Had he really changed his outfit already since they left Space Inc.? *Ridiculous*, McKeyla thought. He pouted at her. "While I appreciate this whole cheeky-spy-girl vibe, I'm safe now, so why don't you just join the fun and give it a rest?"

"Give it a rest?" M said. The prince was pushing her buttons. "Oh, I would, but for *some* reason I actually *care* about saving people's lives, like yours. In fact, I dedicate my own life to studying everything from comparative science to covert operations to investigative methodology to anthropology—not the store—to microbiology, criminology, psychology, to just about any other *-ology* you can think of!"

For once, Prince Xander was speechless. He just stood there staring at her.

"I'm smart," M said. "Get over it."

At that moment, the sound of applause and cheers filtered into the room from the outside.

Prince Xander looked confounded. "Okay, sure that was a good speech, but not quite applause-worthy. . . ."

McKeyla peered over the prince's shoulder to check out the scene outside. A bunch of girls were standing on the front lawn and holding signs that read WE LOVE THE THRILLIONAIRE PRINCE! and MAKE ME YOUR SPACE PRINCESS!

"What are all these people doing here?" M asked worriedly, looking through the blinds.

Bry shrugged. "Beats me. I only posted that I was 'Hanging out with a big-time celeb.' I never said who it was or where."

M crossed her arms over her chest. "NOV8 lesson number two: You don't post from a safe house, because then it isn't, you know, safe. Oh no!" M said as she peered outside.

Cam and Adri inched closer to the window, trying to see what M had seen.

"That's that car again!" Bry said, pointing at the black sedan parked across the street. It was almost hidden by the shrieking fangirls searching for the prince.

M pulled out her notebook. "A.D.I.S.N.—our

location has been compromised. I need you to find an official NOV8 safe house where nobody can find us."

"For you . . . or for you and *those* girls?" A.D.I.S.N. asked pointedly.

"*Now*, A.D.I.S.N.!" M ordered.

The prince watched M as she paced. "Her notebook talks?" he said in disbelief.

Cam nodded. "Pretty sick, huh?"

As A.D.I.S.N. processed the request, the front door of the black sedan opened. A man in a trench coat and sunglasses stepped out and started walking straight toward the house. Bry would've been freaked out, but she was more horrified by his drab outfit.

"Where's the love of color?" she muttered under her breath.

Just then, the man turned, looking right at them. The girls stiffened in fear. When he was almost at the lawn, his hand slipped inside his coat.

"He's reaching for something!" Adri exclaimed.

"We should bolt," added Bry.

"Quick, everyone," M ordered. "Out the back." She stayed behind at the window for a second, aiming her phone at him to take a close-up picture of his face, and then followed.

The girls darted through the house, Prince Xander and his bodyguard right behind them. Jillian struggled to wheel the prince's luggage to the back door. The group ran around the side of the house and hopped into the SUV parked in the driveway. Bry and Adri helped Jillian load the luggage in the back, and they zoomed off down the street.

The man on the front lawn was surprised to hear the car doors slam and turned just in time to watch them leave.

The girls all peered out the back window as the man ran after the SUV. He kept waving his hands and yelling something they couldn't hear.

M turned away and breathed a small sigh of relief. They had gotten the prince out of there and he was still safe.

Her mission was still a success . . . so far.

Chapter Eight
A.R.D.A.*

The safe house had seen better days. M immediately went over to an ancient television to check the news reports.

"Look," said Cam. "There are old cans of beans, dog kibble, and dust."

Adri eyed a bunch of rusty cans in the corner. "Even I wouldn't know what to do with all this, and I'm the best culinary chemist in America."

"That's a thing?" the bodyguard asked.

Adri frowned. "Why does everyone always ask me that?"

*A ROYAL DISAPPEARING ACT

Prince Xander glanced around the dreary room. There were musty curtains covering every window. The walls were paneled with dark wood, and all the furniture smelled of mildew and dust. The prince was not pleased. This was *not* the party he had envisioned. "The fun times just keep getting better. . . ." He blew a big cloud of dust off a can of beans, making M cough.

"You'll have plenty of fun in space," M said, "*if* we can figure out who's after you. We don't have much time."

"How can we help?" Bry asked.

McKeyla was momentarily annoyed but then thought better of it. Maybe they *could* help.

"Get your laptops and meet me in the dining room," M instructed.

The girls spoke over one another.

"Absolutely!"

"Will do!"

Prince Xander crossed his arms over his chest. "Hold on there, chief. If you're busy sleuthing and my staff is busy with various tasks, what am I supposed to do?"

"Oh right!" M said, pretending she cared.

"We can't have a bored blue blood. How 'bout you read a book?"

"I've already read one," the prince replied.

"Guess what, there are more," McKeyla retorted.

"I'm cool, not smart," the prince said with a smirk.

"Fine, then isn't there some space-training exercise you can do?" M asked, pulling her denim jacket closed. She couldn't believe how hopeless the prince was. He couldn't just make himself a snack, or play games on his phone, or watch television like a normal person would? Every minute of every day had to be filled with crazy excitement. It was like entertaining a toddler— one who had an awesome accent.

The prince glanced out the back window. "Sweet! There's a pool. I can practice my water landings. Jillian, get my swim trunks!"

As he made a beeline into the yard, M glanced sideways at the recruits. "He's going to drown, isn't he? Adri, keep an eye on him."

Adri nodded dutifully, following the prince out to the pool. Cam and Bry researched news articles online about the prince's launch while McKeyla worked with A.D.I.S.N., pulling up the photo she took of their suspect. She zoomed in on his face and outfit, looking for possible clues. She noticed a familiar star logo on his coat.

"That dude's car and his jacket had the same emblem on them," M said.

"Plus he was creepy," Cam said.

"Super creepy," Bry added.

M pulled up NOV8's image search, cutting and pasting the emblem inside. It started scanning through hundreds of images. After a few minutes, she had a match. "It appears the insignia in question is the corporate logo of an international cyber-security firm known as Black Star."

"Black Star? Sounds dark and pointy," Cam joked.

M scratched her head. She knew she'd heard that name somewhere, but where?

"Black Star . . ." she mumbled. "Isn't that the company that just donated all those computers to Africa?"

"Maybe," Bry said, pulling up several windows

on her computer. There were hundreds of controversial articles related to the organization. "It seems like they've been in the news a *ton*."

Bry opened a video of a recent press conference. A stern yet richly handsome man wearing a crisp blue suit stood behind the podium. FRANCOIS DARONE, CEO was displayed on the banner at the bottom of the screen.

"We're pleased to announce the next phase in Black Star's growth," the commanding CEO stated. "This IPO affords us the resources to continue our commitment to the process of technology and the protection of our users' private data. Thank you."

As Mr. Darone talked, M spotted a familiar face in the background. "Wait, pause it! Right there! See that?"

"It's the creepy guy!" Bry said.

M pulled Bry's laptop toward her, cropping the frame so the image was just the man's face. Then she inputted it into A.D.I.S.N.'s face-recognition program. The screen flashed through hundreds of passport photos, trying to match the man's features to one in the database.

Finally, it stopped on a picture very similar to the one they had. AARON MARKUS, it read.

Cam leaned in, reading his data. "Senior-level black ops? And now he's chief director of operations for Black Star."

"Think, M, think. . . ." M said to herself. "Why would a major cyber-security company want to kidnap the prince or stop his flight?"

Cam and Bry also leaned in, studying the information. Bry was about to run a web search on him when they heard loud, thumping music coming from outside. The girls headed into the backyard to find the prince leisurely floating on a blue raft in the middle of the pool. There were a dozen people in the backyard, some dipping their feet in the water, others lying on the lounge chairs, drinking iced tea, or flirting with the prince. Inflatable palm trees and beach balls were scattered everywhere.

"What's going on here?" M asked. "Where's Adri?"

"The neighbors wanted to come over for a swim!" Prince Xander said, paddling around. "Couldn't very well say no. That wouldn't be a very neighborly thing to do. Well, at least I don't think it is. I don't have neighbors—I live in a castle." He winked.

M balled her hands into fists. "Ugh! Keep a close eye on the party prince. I'm going to go find Adri."

She took off through the house, trying to figure out (1) where Adri was and (2) why she wasn't watching the prince like M had told her to. Now there were a dozen strangers hanging in the yard of an NOV8 safe house! Not only had he compromised the integrity of the house, but any one of them could also be working for Black Star! They were all complete strangers who hadn't been properly screened. McKeyla was all about the rules, especially when civilian lives are at risk and she was the one in charge.

She turned a corner, running into Jillian, who was talking frantically on her cell, snapping, "I told you I'll take care of it!" She hung up as soon as she saw M, her face pale. "Um, does the prince need something?" she stammered.

"Have you seen Adri?" M asked her. Jillian shook her head and M kept searching the other rooms of the house. No Adri. When she finally went back outside, she found Adri, Cam, and Bry huddled around a table filled with bowls of colorful liquid.

"Now I just pull the alginate strands out of the calcium lactate bath," Adri narrated as she squirted one liquid into a bowl. She then held up long, thin strips of red noodles that had formed. "Molecular noodles! *¡Ya está!*"

Cam ate a forkful. "Looks like spaghetti, tastes like strawberries. Yum!"

"Pretty brilliant, huh?" Adri asked.

While the crowd oohed and aahed, M scanned the rest of the backyard. There was an empty raft . . . an empty chair . . . an empty table. No prince.

"Where'd he go?" she asked, trying to appear calm.

Cam turned around, staring at the empty pool. "He was floating there a second ago. . . ."

"I started cooking and . . ." Adri admitted, looking stricken.

"We got a little distracted," Bry said guiltily.

Cam hung her head. All three knew they had screwed up.

M wasted no more time and darted into the

house, checking every room again. No prince, Jillian, security guards, or car. They were all gone. The girls caught up to M in the empty driveway.

"What are we going to do?" Cam asked.

"I think you've done enough," M snapped. She angrily stashed away her notebook and computer and zipped her bag up while the girls watched, unsure what was happening. "It was *my* job to protect the prince and I failed. I failed everybody in every way! If anything happens to him, it's all *my* fault."

"You can't blame yourself," Bry said kindly.

M lost her temper and threw her hands up. "Yes, Bry, I can. You know why?" she yelled. The girls cringed. "Because I *knew* I was better off handling this case by *myself*. It's obvious the three of you would rather mess around than get serious. None of you have what it takes to be a real agent. Not one! Now *I'm* going to find the prince and take care of this myself, just like I should have done in the first place!"

With that, M stormed off down the street. Cam, Bry, and Adri looked at one another in dismay. They'd never seen M so mad. They knew they had messed up big time. Why hadn't they kept at least one eye on the prince during Adri's experiment? Why had Adri stepped away to find all those ingredients? And why had Bry posted on social media? It'd probably led the bad guys right to them.

Then there was the hardest question of all, the one they couldn't bring themselves to think about. . . .

Was this the end? Did it mean they'd never get to work for NOV8?

Chapter Nine
M.M.H.S.T.*

M sat in her secret closet lab, staring intently at the holographic computer map in front of her, searching for any sign of the prince's car. She had to find a clue of where they'd taken him. She spotted several black cars in the vicinity of the safe house, but it was impossible to tell which one his was. She ran a few social media searches, trying to figure out if anyone had tweeted or posted a sighting. McKeyla was hitting dead ends in every direction.

"I'm sorry," M said remorsefully, glancing up at the Quail on the screen. "I tried my best

*McKEYLA McALISTER HAS SECOND THOUGHTS

to work with those girls, and now I've lost the prince. This never would've happened if my attention wasn't diverted by them. . . . They were so unfocused and unreliable."

"Don't forget uncool," A.D.I.S.N. chimed in from the desk.

"No," the Quail corrected. "They're three exceptional high school students who can still help you."

"Yes, they're smart," M agreed, watching the map. "But they're not operatives. If I don't find the prince and this launch fails, I'll never forgive myself."

The Quail just nodded sympathetically. At this point in her career, she was much better than M at handling stressful situations. Twenty years in NOV8 made her a seasoned veteran, and she'd learned that the only way to handle a crisis was to remain calm so she could think clearly.

"I understand that things didn't go as planned, but it's not too late," she said. "Let those girls assist you so you can find him. Everyone makes mistakes during training. Remember your little mishap with the Bengal tiger?"

McKeyla cringed. "I thought we were never going to talk about the tiger. . . ."

"I deleted it from all the records!" A.D.I.S.N. called out in her supportive, high-pitched electronic voice. She wanted McKeyla to know how much she did for her.

"My point is," the Quail went on, "*you* weren't always this professional and responsible, either."

M shook her head. "It's not that I expect them to be like me . . . but they're not even *close* to being like me. They just couldn't handle it."

The Quail tilted her head to one side, giving M a hard look. "McKeyla . . . do you *really* believe you gave them a fair chance?"

M let out a deep breath. Maybe she *had* been kind of harsh with them. Bry was technically the one who'd hacked into the security guard's monitor to distract him—which was the only reason why they'd gotten into the hangar. Cam had built that police scanner, and Adri had been the one who'd gotten them past the prince's bodyguard. It was not like they hadn't helped at all.

She remembered their faces when she'd left, how shocked and sorry they'd looked. Was her mom right?

"Maybe you have a point. . . ." M admitted. "I didn't give them a fair chance. Maybe they were trying and I didn't know how to lead them." She suddenly turned on herself. "What's wrong with me? Why am I so stubborn? So difficult . . . so annoying? Was I born this way?"

"Nooooo, sweetie," the Quail said, almost too quickly. "I mean, no, Agent McAlister, you were not born that way. But why don't we talk about this later, after you get the girls and find the prince?"

M couldn't stop, though. It was like all these thoughts and feelings were coming to the surface, and she had to collect them before they floated away.

"I guess I just want people to do things my way, or I just do it myself. Maybe I shouldn't be so closed off. Let people in, let them help me . . ."

"Great idea for the future. Time is ticking. . . ." the Quail admonished, trying to get M back on track.

"Just open my eyes and not be so oblivious to the world around me," M went on. "See what's right in front of my—"

Just then, she spun her chair to the side and

caught sight of the monitor to her left. Cam, Bry, and Adri were all hovered around the camera in the safe house, waving and trying to get M's attention. She could tell from their flapping lips and flailing arms that they were yelling something to her, but the speakers weren't on. She tapped the keyboard.

"You guys? What's going on?" M asked.

"We got him!" they cried in unison.

The girls moved away from the camera, revealing the dining room of the safe house. Aaron Markus was sitting in a chair behind them. His arms and legs were strapped to the seat, and wires wound around his body. He had a piece of tape over his mouth. He struggled against his bonds—he wanted to talk, badly.

"I can't believe it!" M shouted, covering her smile with her hand.

The girls started dancing around the room, singing and high-fiving. "*Go, us . . . go, us . . .*" they chanted.

"Mission *no imposible*!" Adri yelled, folding in some Spanish the way she always did when she was really excited.

"Great job. So . . ." M said, visually scanning the room behind them, "where's the prince?"

The girls all stopped dancing. Bry smiled sheepishly.

"Uh . . ." she said, winding one of her long black curls around her finger. "We forgot to ask."

M let out a small laugh. Okay, so they weren't perfect, but they had found the suspect and detained him. That was major.

"I'll be right there!" M assured them. She grabbed her hat and A.D.I.S.N., and headed for the door.

Chapter Ten
T.W.T.A.N.B.T.T.*

As soon as M got to the safe house, Cam and Adri caught her up on the details. Apparently, after she'd left earlier, the girls had stayed, trying to figure out what to do next. That was when they noticed the black car outside. Aaron, their dubious suspect, started walking toward the house.

Thinking fast, they hid right behind the front door, jumping out as soon as he came in. They said he'd been caught so off guard it only took them a minute to tie him up.

*THE WHOLE TRUTH AND NOTHING BUT THE TRUTH

M stood back, observing Bry as she hooked up some sort of homemade device to two of the suspect's fingers. Bry then connected the red and green wires to a breath mint box. M leaned over, inspecting the intriguing device.

"Uh . . . why are you connecting him to a tin of curiously strong mints?" she asked.

"It's my cleverly disguised portable lie detector," Bry explained, talking at twice normal speed, even for her. "It flashes green if you're telling the truth and red when you're lying."

"Or if you have really bad breath," Cam joked. She pushed her dark red hair off her shoulders.

Bry opened the lid of the mint tin, revealing an intricate web of wires. She looked down at the suspect. "Now, tell us what you did with the prince," she said, suddenly very gruff.

"And about Black Star's secret plan!" Cam added.

"Don't worry, girls," Adri said, stepping forward. She smacked a pink spatula in her hand, her lips attempting a menacing sneer. "I'm going to get some answers out of our new friend here. I just hope I don't have to use any unsavory methods. But that's entirely up to you, *chico.* . . ."

M ripped the tape from his mouth, allowing him to speak. He had thin brown hair and a brown beard, some of which, painfully and accidentally, had come off with the tape. *Oops!*

"Yes, yes, I work for Black Star," he said, trying to catch his breath. "But it's not what you think."

Bry peered at the lights on the side of the tin. *Ding.* The green light flashed. "He's telling the truth!"

"I've been trying to warn you," Aaron said. *Ding.*

"Warn us?" Adri yelled, brandishing her spatula. "About what? Your evil plot to kidnap the prince?"

"Nobody's been kidnapped," Aaron said, looking at them with his suspicious, beady black eyes. "Black Star isn't after the prince; they're after data. They're planting an illegal hacking device in the prince's luggage." *Ding.*

The girls exchanged confused looks. Nobody was kidnapped? They needed to get to the bottom of this, fast.

"What do you mean, a 'hacking device'?" Bry asked.

"It's the only one of its kind," Aaron said. "They're going to use it to hack into a government satellite up there. This isn't about the prince at all; he's just a foil to hide their real intentions." *Ding.*

"What about the phone call?" Cam asked. "Someone called Space Inc. and warned them to keep the prince off that flight."

"That was me!" Aaron said, obviously frustrated. "I've been trying to do whatever I can to get this launch canceled. If that device goes onto that ship, Black Star will be able to steal millions of people's personal information. I never thought Black Star was capable of this. Darone made us believe he was an innovator and humanitarian who wanted to do great things with his technology. But it was all lies." *Ding.* He was still telling them the truth!

But there was one question Adri just couldn't get out of her head. "Why not go to the *policía*?"

"I tried," Aaron said. *BZZT.*

"Lie!" Bry held up the lie detector. It was flashing red now.

Adri lifted the pink spatula, threatening to whack him on the nose.

"Okay, okay!" Aaron cried. "The truth is I'm scared of Darone and what he'd do to me if he found out." *Ding.*

"But why would an Internet security giant want to steal anyone's personal data?" M asked, still puzzling over the plot.

"Why else?" Aaron scoffed. "Greed. Darone wants as much personal info as he can get his slimy hands on so he can sell it for billions." *Ding.*

"Personal info?" Cam asked. "You mean, like, all our e-mails and contacts?"

"Photos and texts . . ." Adri added.

Bry gasped thinking of all her social media posts.

"Yeah, all that stuff," Aaron confirmed.

"I think I'm going to be sick," Bry said weakly.

"We have to stop them!" M exclaimed.

Cam noticed the television set that was still on. She pointed at the news report. "It looks like we might be too late. . . ."

The prince was standing at the launch site, waving to the cameras. He was already in his spacesuit with the spacecraft behind him.

"Cam, call your dad. . . ." M said.

Cam whipped out her cell and dialed, but it just rang and rang. "Voice mail. He's gotta be in the control room already. No way I can reach him now."

"The hacking device!" M cried, getting an idea. "If we can find a way into Space Inc., we can stop it from getting onto that spacecraft."

"I say we destroy it so Black Star won't be able to harm anyone," Cam said. The girls nodded, agreeing with the plan. But if they were going to have a shot at pulling it off, they had no time to waste.

M paused at the door. "There's one thing I still don't get. If nobody kidnapped the prince, then who took him from the safe house to the launch?"

Cam thought about the prince and the entourage who followed him everywhere. He had three security guards, a bodyguard, and a personal assistant with him. "I bet one of his staff is working with them. . . ."

"A mole?" Bry asked.

"A dirty, rotten mole!" Adri agreed. Oh, how she'd like to use her spatula on them!

M let out a deep breath, mad at herself for not realizing it before. "And I have a feeling I know exactly who it is. Come on. Let's go!"

"Who?" Bry asked as they started to the door. "Who is it?"

But M had more pressing things on her mind . . . like finding and deactivating that destructive device!

Chapter Eleven
B.A.E.T.S.T.W.A.W.K.I.*

Bry pushed through the crowd of screaming fans, moving closer to the massive spacecraft. She stood on her tippy-toes. "There he is!" she said, pointing to the prince, who was mugging for the crowd. He was standing on the stairs in front of the ship, about to address hundreds of excited fans in front of him, his blue Space Inc. jumpsuit zipped up to his chin. The row in front of the stage was all teen girls, some holding signs, others wearing T-shirts that read I'M OVER THE MOON FOR PRINCE XANDER. It seemed like everywhere

*BREAKING AND ENTERING TO SAVE THE WORLD AS WE KNOW IT

they turned there were security guards and barricades, holding the huge noisy crowd back.

"I want to thank all you awesome people for coming here today as I embark on this epic journey," he said, looking at the news cameras lined up in the front row. His crew stood beside him, all wearing similar blue jumpsuits. "A real, live, once-in-a-lifetime historic event," he said, pumping his fist in the air, and all the fangirls screamed.

McKeyla led the girls around the side of the crowd, toward the central building. "Well, there's one saving grace today," she whispered. "We don't have to listen to the rest of his speech."

They snuck around the side of the main building, looking at the security guard stationed in the lobby, right in front of a giant metal sculpture.

"We have to figure out how to get inside the rest of the building to find the device," M said.

"Maybe it's time for a little explosion," Adri said, peering into her bag of tricks. "I have all the ingredients." M was impressed that Adri was so prepared. She wondered how deep that purse must be!

"You handle the explosion, I'll handle the distraction," Cam said with a wink. She led Bry up to the security desk while M and Adri stayed behind. "Hey there, George!" she said loudly, acting super peppy. "How's my favorite security guard ever? This is my friend Bryden. We just wanted to wish my dad luck before the launch."

The security guard shook his head. "I'm afraid the building is on full lockdown. No visitors during pre-launch time."

"Awww, man," Cam moaned with exaggerated disappointment. "You're kidding. I was really hoping to see—"

BLAM!

They turned around to see thick hot-pink foam covering the metal sculpture in the center of the lobby. Adri and M were hiding behind a nearby plant.

George rushed over to the sculpture, not sure how to clean up the mess. He looked panicked. While he inspected the damage, with pink foam dripping all over, Cam reached over his desk and pressed the button that unlocked the main doors. Then they all slipped into the building.

"I thought you said a *little* eruption?" Cam said as Adri ran past her.

"I might have overshot it a bit. . . ." Adri smiled as she tried to keep up in her heels.

The girls ran down the hallway, deeper into the main building. There were signs everywhere warning AUTHORIZED PERSONNEL ONLY and SECURE AREA. They turned left and hit a dead end with three marked doors. One read MISSION CONTROL, another TELEMETRY, and the third FINAL LAUNCH ASSEMBLY.

"So, Bryden Bandweth from Maywood Glen," Adri said, talking in a deep voice as if she were a game show host, "do you pick door number one, door number two, or door number three?"

"Ooohhhh, I don't know. I like the number one, but two could be twice as good. . . ." Before Bry could ramble on any further, an alarm sounded. George must've discovered their break-in and alerted the other guards.

"Door number three it is!" McKeyla decided quickly.

Cam tried the door, but it was locked. She studied the panel beside it. "It's a voice-recognition lock," she said. "An authorized voice is the only way that door opens."

"This is the perfect job for A.D.I.S.N.," M said, pulling out her notebook. "She matches voices flawlessly."

"Aw, love you, too, bestie!" said A.D.I.S.N.

Cam took out her phone and played a saved voice mail from her dad. A.D.I.S.N. recorded every word, then listened to Cam's command on what to say and how. M held her notebook up to the door.

"Charles Coyle," A.D.I.S.N. said, mimicking Mr. Coyle's voice. "Access code: Echo Mike Charlie Two."

The door buzzed open. All four girls ran inside, but they didn't get more than a few feet before they were in total darkness. M and Cam pulled out their cell phones, illuminating the space in front of them.

It was a long corridor with a steel door at the other end. Bry began to step forward in the darkness.

M grabbed her before Bry could go another inch. She was staring at a pinpoint of red light in the distance. "Adri . . . got any baking soda left?"

"Am I a culinary chemist or what?" Adri reached into her purse, grabbed a fistful of baking soda, and blew it into the air. Instantly, the girls could see an intricate web of red lasers, crisscrossing the room in all directions, leaving no space to walk or even crawl through. If they hit any of the beams, they would set off the alarm.

"How do we get through that?" Bry asked.

Adri, Bry, and McKeyla stared ahead, their stomachs tightening. They'd come all this way just to get stopped by a bunch of laser beams? Was this really how their night was going to end?

But Cam didn't even hesitate.

"Compact mirror?" she said, holding out her hand to Adri. Adri dug through her bag, finally surrendering her double-mirrored compact.

"Gum?" Cam said, holding out her hand to Bry, who reluctantly spit out her chewed-up gum.

"It still has flavor!" Bry protested.

Cam pulled her skateboard off her back and put it on the floor. She set the gum on the front, and pressed the compact down on top of it, securing it in place. Then she readjusted the compact's tiny mirror, checking and rechecking the angle to make sure she got it right.

"If it's exactly three-point-five-seven meters away, with an angle of approximately forty-five degrees, the velocity should be . . . Okay . . . here goes. . . ."

Cam took a deep breath, hoping the calculation she did in her head was right. She carefully rolled the skateboard forward, finally letting it slip from her grasp. As it glided across the room, they all held their breath. It slowly rolled to a stop right in front of the metal box with the bright red laser emitters. The laser beams were captured and bounced back between the two mirrored halves of the compact. Now the girls could pass through!

"Nailed it!" Cam said, pumping her fist in the air. Adri gave her friend a high five as Bry and McKeyla looked on. They had just thwarted one of the most complex security systems in the country with only a piece of gum, a skateboard, and a mirror!

As the girls ran to the steel door, Adri let out a small yip of excitement. Right in front of them was an access panel that required a number code. Bry flipped open her laptop, then connected a cable to a remote circuit board in the laptop and electrical clips inside the panel's electronic lock system.

"I love number games. . . ." She smiled. This was the perfect chance to put all her electronics expertise to work. All those nights she'd stayed up late coding just for fun were totally worth it.

Then she hit her Random Number Generator application, and the screen started flipping through thousands of four-digit combinations. It ran for a few minutes, then stopped on 3421. The lock turned and the door popped open.

"Ding! Ding!" Bry said. "We have a winner!"

The girls let out a collective sigh of relief. They were just seconds away from finding Black Star's hacking device. The girls could practically hear the clock ticking down as they raced through the door. They had to reach the prince's luggage before it was too late!

They ran as fast as they could, winding through a long hallway to the Launch Assembly Room. It was vast with huge ceilings and mechanical equipment on two of the four walls. Far across the hangar, people in white suits and masks were doing last-minute checks on the spacecraft. Adri spotted the prince's luggage on a plastic mat a few feet away, waiting to be loaded into the craft. The girls darted toward the pile, hoping the hacking device was still inside.

The girls began unzipping the dozen suit-cases—how many outfits did the prince need for space, anyway?—searching for the device. They found tube after tube of hair sculpting goop and a dozen pairs of designer jeans, but nothing that looked like what Aaron had described. Where was this menacing device that could destroy the world?

Adri was going through a duffel bag filled with video games when she heard McKeyla gasp. All the girls turned to look.

"Got it!" M said, pulling a large black box with cables out of a black suitcase. An LCD display was at the top of it, showing the radio frequency, the distance and power setting, and an IP address.

Bry studied the device. It was the most sophisticated piece of equipment she'd ever seen, with a glass front that made its internal system visible. "It's a transmitter and antenna," she said, moved by its complexity. "No doubt with state-of-the-art hacking software inside. A beautiful piece of technology," she added, wiping away a tear.

"Yeah, yeah," M said. "It's gorgeous. Now, let's kill it. Fast!"

She glanced back, where a few of the Space Inc. workers were. They'd spotted the girls across the hangar. One man put his radio to his mouth, calling for security. She knew what they must look like—a bunch of fangirls trying to get a glimpse of the prince. They only had a few minutes before they would be swarmed by guards.

"We need a power source strong enough to short out its core drive," Bry explained, talking twice as fast as she normally did.

Cam opened up the front of the device, exposing the wires, circuitry, and a battery. She attached one short electrical cable to a power source in the wall of the hangar and pulled a longer electrical cable (the longest she had) from the bag of tech tricks that had served them so well this far, but, unspooling it, she realized to her dismay that it was still too short to reach any power supply on the wall. And they dared not move the device, not knowing if or how it might be booby-trapped.

"There's no way to complete the circuit," she said, pointing to the device. "We still need about ten feet of wire to connect back to the device."

McKeyla turned, watching as George and three security guards rushed in through the far exit. The girls scanned the hangar. They were running out of time—if they didn't destroy the device before security reached them, it might never be destroyed. What if it fell into the wrong hands?

"How about us?" M said, looking at the distance between the device and the power source. "We can conduct electricity."

"You're right," Bry agreed. "We can complete the circuit using our bodies instead of the wire! It will send just enough power to prematurely activate the device now. We could confuse it so it shorts itself out and causes a circuit failure."

"It won't hurt us?" Adri asked.

"Nope! Since the battery is low voltage, the current is so small we won't even feel it," Bry replied.

"Yeah, just no fingers in sockets or grabbing power lines, please!" Cam said with a wink.

"Who's ready to make a human chain?" M asked, holding out her hand.

Cam clipped into the device, then stretched out her hand. The girls clasped hands one by one to form a human chain from Cam to Adri to M to Bry. With her free hand, Bry reached out and grabbed the wire connected to the power source. They all watched as the device lit up. It made a few whirring sounds, like it was working, then a fuse blew. Smoke filled the air.

Cam leaned over, looking at the LCD display. It read, CIRCUIT FAILURE.

"It worked!" M said. "We did it! Go, us!"

The girls broke into a celebratory dance. They hooted and high-fived, singing *"Go, us . . . go, us"*—and this time even M joined in. They were so excited it took them a few seconds to notice the pack of security guards closing in on them. Cam looked up and saw her father walking toward them from the far end of the hangar. He looked worried, and a bit angry, too.

"Cam, what are you doing here?" he said in his most stern *you've got some explaining to do* voice.

Cam felt her throat tighten, the way it always did when she was trying not to cry. She'd been so caught up in stopping Black Star that she'd forgotten that she'd also deceived her father's coworker, vandalized his workplace, and broke through every security system in the east wing of Space Inc. How could she possibly tell him everything that had happened in the last two days? Would he believe her?

"We can explain, Dad," she said, taking a deep breath. "I promise. . . ."

Chapter Twelve
W.T.T.S.S.*

Francois Darone, the CEO of Black Star, looked down at the control in his hand. Just seconds before, everything had been on track. The hacking device had been responding, but now it read CONNECTION OFFLINE. FAILURE kept blinking over and over again.

"What happened?" he growled at Jillian, who was standing behind him, watching the launch. "What's going on?"

Before Jillian could answer, they heard the *Whoop! Whoop!* of a police car. He turned to see the four girls marching toward them. The massive crowd parted as they came closer. Mr. Coyle, George, and a team of security guards were right behind them, along with a security vehicle with flashing red lights.

Hundreds of people turned to watch as McKeyla and her friends walked right up to Jillian, the prince's assistant, and Francois Darone, who were both standing in the front row, waiting for the launch. Darone looked just a bit less polished than he had five minutes ago.

McKeyla had confronted bad guys before—thieves and liars and people who'd tried to sabotage NOV8's efforts. But this felt different. Darone was out for world domination. He might have been the most deceitful, villainous bad guy yet.

"We stopped you, Darone," M said, trying to keep her voice even. She balled her hands into fists. "You and Black Star can't hurt anyone anymore."

"Yeah, your device is *tostada*!" Adri scoffed. "Burnt toast. So burnt you can't even scrape off the black part with a knife and still eat it."

"You'll find the carcass inside." Cam smiled, pointing back toward the hangar.

Darone sneered at the four teenage girls in front of him. He kept looking at the security team, then Mr. Coyle, his brows drawn together as if to say *Why are you listening to these girls?*

"This is ridiculous," he snapped. "I don't know what you're talking about. Why would anyone believe a bunch of silly young girls?"

Mr. Coyle stepped forward. "*I* believe them. And it's all true. Every word of it. We've got the device, and these girls stopped it."

Cam smiled up at her dad. After she'd explained about Aaron Markus, Black Star, and the hacking device—he didn't need any other proof. Sure, maybe he and George wished the girls hadn't spewed pink sludge all over the Space Inc. lobby, but considering the circumstances, even that could be forgiven.

"Take him away," George called out as a group of security guards rushed in. They handcuffed Darone and put him in the back of the police car.

"Call the lawyers!" Darone shouted as he

ducked inside. "Jillian, call the lawyers! What are you waiting for?"

M started toward Jillian. This whole time the prince's assistant had been against him, working with Black Star to try to download millions of dollars' worth of personal information. How could she wake up every morning and smile, pretending to be someone she wasn't?

"And Jillian . . ." she said, angrier now, "all those secret phone calls, how you had the prince leave the safe house—I knew there was something off about you, but I never imagined you could be involved in such an evil plan."

Prince Xander came down the stairs from the podium where he had been standing, a stunned look on his face. It took him a few seconds to process what was going on. "Jillian? A mole? No wonder you stank at your job. . . ."

As the guards began handcuffing her, Jillian sneered at the girls. "You nosy little spy girls think you're so smart, don't you?" she asked, struggling against the guards. "Ever since I took that stupid job with the prince, it's been 'Get this, Jillian!' or 'Get that, Jillian!' Darone offered me the chance to have money, power—to be the boss for once. But you girls had to go and ruin it. I won't forget this. Or you, Agent McAlister! You can tell that stupid organization you work with that they'll regret the day they messed with me."

"Yeah," M said. "We'll tell them you send your love . . . from jail!"

The girls watched as the guards put Jillian into another squad car. They high-fived and bumped fists, then threw their arms around one another like a real team. They were so excited about solving the case that they didn't notice Prince Xander walking toward them.

"I can't leave without apologizing to you, M," Prince Xander said, stepping up to her. He was so close she could see the flecks of blue in his eyes. She had to admit—he *was* kind of cute.

"I gave you a hard time from the minute we met," he went on. "You didn't deserve that."

"Wow, I don't know what to say. . . ." M smirked. "Wait, yes, I do. You're right! I actually know what I'm talking about!"

"Yes, you do," Prince Xander laughed. "Despite every stupid thing I did to get in your way, you and those clever girls still managed to save the world. You're obviously a great leader."

M smiled at her shoes, trying not to look him in the eye. She could feel the heat rising in her cheeks. Was she actually blushing like a Prince Xander fangirl? If she kept this up, it wouldn't be long before she was wearing one of those I'M OVER THE MOON FOR PRINCE XANDER shirts.

"I try to be a good influence. . . ." she said.

"Well, it worked on them, and it worked on me."

"Oh really? How's that?" she asked.

"You make me want to read a book."

"Awwww," M said. "Not a picture book, right?"

"No, one with lots of tiny words."

"Welcome to the smart side," she laughed. "Well . . . have a safe trip. Enjoy battling aliens with laser swords. . . ."

He winked at her, then turned to go. "I'll catch you when I get back, M."

She stood there, watching as he climbed the podium. Yes, Prince Xander was pompous, and in love with himself, and had the attention span of a toddler on a sugar high, but he was also kind of . . . sort of . . . sweet?

M pushed away the thought, trying to be professional about the situation. This was business, after all.

M turned to the girls, who were standing beside her, giggling. Bry was bouncing up and down on her toes, the way she always did when she was excited. Did she just see the prince wink at M? So lucky!

The crowd watched as Prince Xander walked off toward the spacecraft. Music blared. Some people waved glow sticks in the air. Others shouted and cheered, watching as the shuttle rumbled and whirred to life.

The launch clock above the podium ticked down. There was only a minute left, then thirty seconds, then the entire crowd was counting down:

Five . . . four . . . three . . . two . . . one . . .

Smoke billowed out from under the rocket. The ground rumbled and shook. Adri, Cam, and Bry had their arms around one another as they stood there, looking up at the sky. Everywhere they turned, people were clapping and cheering. M smiled up at the spaceship as it lifted off, the fire propelling it into the atmosphere, far beyond where they could see. She couldn't have imagined a more beautiful sight.

Chapter Thirteen
S.I.T.N.C.[*]

Back at M's lab, the girls were smushed together on the couch, watching the footage of the space launch for the third time. A reporter narrated the scene as the spacecraft prepared to blast into the sky. "Prince Xander's space launch this evening was a huge success," he said. "All thanks to an elusive group of four girls who helped Space Inc. thwart a dangerous, last-minute threat."

The spacecraft took off, disappearing into the atmosphere. "I can watch that launch a zillion times and never get bored," Cam said, leaning her head on Adri's shoulder.

Bry sat up straight, her eyes wide. She was gripping her cell phone in her hand. "Prince Xander just posted a video from space!"

She held up the screen, showing the other girls. The prince was floating in the spacecraft. He'd put the letters S.I.T.N.C. across the video.

"S.I.T.N.C.?" Cam asked.

"That's easy." M smiled. "Smart Is The New Cool."

The girls all high-fived M, thrilled that she was finally breaking the code. There was hope for her yet! As they celebrated the small victory, the monitor over the desk turned on, revealing a video chat with the Quail.

"Congratulations, Agent McAlister, on closing the case of Prince Xander," the Quail said.

"Thanks, but I didn't do it alone," M said. "I had help . . . from my friends." She glanced around at the girls, smiling.

"OMG, what did you call them?" A.D.I.S.N. demanded.

"Sorry, A.D.I.S.N., they *are* my friends," M said, standing her ground. Then she softened. "Just like you." She looked at the girls. "And not only that, you're all first-rate operatives, and I'm proud to say I've had the honor of working with each and every one of you."

Bry clapped her hand over her mouth. "I can't believe you just said that!"

"Me neither," A.D.I.S.N. sniped.

"Believe it, A.D.I.S.N.," M said.

"Well, you know what they say," A.D.I.S.N. said, "any friends of yours . . . are friends of yours. That I can try to be nicer to."

"Not sure that's an actual saying, but I appreciate the sentiment," M laughed. Then she turned to her mom. "You were right about this whole team thing. I know I'm scheduled to leave for my next assignment, but if you and NOV8 approve, I'd like to stay here so we can keep working together."

Cam glanced sideways at Adri and Bry. To have M here all year long, building experiments and helping them continue their training . . . it was better than anything they could've imagined. They waited, watching the Quail's face to see how she'd respond.

"Affirmative," the Quail finally said. "NOV8 will allow Maywood Glen to be your interim base of operations."

The girls let out a few excited yelps. Adri, Cam, and Bry all hugged M, and for the first time she hugged them back. She smushed them so hard no one could breathe.

"This is how you do it, right?" M asked. She was always so awkward with hugs, like she didn't quite know how to be as mushy as they wanted her to be.

"Ouch, in a good way," Cam laughed.

"Maybe loosen up on the stranglehold?" Bry asked.

McKcyla laughed along with them, feeling for the first time like she actually belonged somewhere. She didn't have to pack her luggage the next day and leave for another mission. She could stay right here, in this house, hanging out with Adri, Bry, and Cam every day after school.

She glanced around, looking at the walls where she'd hung some of the papers and evidence from the mission. What would it be like for this to be a real home like Bry's, with family photos everywhere, and friends coming over to hang out and scarf down everything in the fridge?

Amazing, she thought. *It would be amazing.*

Epilogue

Bry leaned toward her friends. "I.S.C.B.T.P.S.U.
A.M.F.O.S."

Cam just shrugged. "Yeah, I Still Can't
Believe The Prince Sent Us A Message From
Outer Space, either."

M couldn't believe Cam had figured that one
out. Had the girls hidden some secret decoder
somewhere? Had they rehearsed these before-
hand? They were either psychic or out of their
minds—either way, they had to teach her how
to do it, too.

"Come on," M begged. "You guys have to teach me how you do those crazy long ones!"

"As long as you keep teaching us secret-agenting . . ." Bry smiled.

M glanced behind them, making sure no one had heard. "NOV8 lesson number three," she said. "You might not want to keep shouting out that you're a secret agent."

"Got it," Bry said, her voice barely a whisper.

"When do you think we'll get our next assignment?" Cam asked. It hadn't even been two days since the space launch and she was already itching for a new mission, and a chance to use more of her crazy inventions (even if they didn't have very good names).

Just then, A.D.I.S.N.'s voice sounded from M's notebook. "Girls, it's time for your next mission."

"That was quick," Adri chirped.

"This is awesome," Cam breathed.

"I'msoexcitedIcan'tstandit!" Bry said, her words blending together.

"Let do this," Adri added.

McKeyla turned toward her new friends.

She opened the notebook, to A.D.I.S.N.'s screen, and they leaned in until the glow was illuminating their faces. They had their arms around each other, ready to tackle whatever came next. From now on, they were in this together—a team. "What do you say?" McKeyla asked. "Are you in?"

Then they peered down at the notebook, smiling as they read the details of their next mission.

MOLECULAR SPAGHETTI EXPERIMENT

LAB SUPPLIES:

- 1 teaspoon (5 grams) sodium alginate powder (available online or at specialty chef stores)
- Water
- 2L plastic soda bottle
- Squeeze bottle
- Food coloring
- Sugar
- Powdered drink mix (like Kool-Aid®)
- Large bowl
- 1 tablespoon (15 grams) calcium lactate powder (available online or at specialty chef stores)

INSTRUCTIONS:

Create an alginate solution by mixing 1 teaspoon sodium alginate powder and 1 cup of water. Use the tips below for best results.

Tips for dissolving sodium alginate

Sodium alginate can take a while to dissolve. Follow these steps for best results:

1. Pour 1 cup (8 oz.) of water into a soda bottle. Then quickly add in 1 teaspoon of sodium alginate.
2. Cap the soda bottle, and shake it as hard as you can. It's workout time! Shake for three to five minutes.

3. Let the soda bottle sit for 1 hour so tiny bubbles come out. The liquid should thicken.

Pour the alginate solution into the squeeze bottle. Put a drop of food coloring into the bottle if you want your molecular spaghetti to have some color. Add a bit of sugar or powdered drink mix for sweetness and flavor. Mix together. (Adri made strawberry and blueberry—yum!)

In a large bowl, dissolve 1 tablespoon of calcium lactate into 1 cup of water. Now squirt the alginate solution into the bowl, wait 30 seconds, and *¡Ya está!* you have molecular spaghetti!

PICKING UP S.T.E.A.M.

with Science, Technology, Engineering, Art & Math:

Pretty much everything around us is made of molecules. Some molecules are special because they can link together into chains. When they are floating around on their own, we call them "monomers," and when they are linked, we call them "polymers." Mixing the two liquids causes some of the molecules to link together, making molecular spaghetti!

MAKE YOUR OWN "WATERFALL"

LAB SUPPLIES:

- ◆ Two flasks, or similar short and clear containers
- ◆ A couple of books
- ◆ Water
- ◆ Paper towel
- ◆ Food coloring (optional)

INSTRUCTIONS:

On a table, put one flask on top of a couple of books. Fill three-fourths of the flask with water. Put one end of a paper towel into the flask until it reaches the bottom. Put the second flask directly onto the surface of the table near the first flask. Put the other end of the paper towel into this empty flask so that it touches the bottom, too. Check back every fifteen minutes until the water has "fallen" from one flask to the other. Try putting food coloring in the water at the beginning of the experiment and see what happens.

PICKING UP S.T.E.A.M.

with Science, Technology, Engineering, Art & Math:

How can water move from one flask into another through a paper towel? Sounds like a magic trick, but it's science. Paper towels absorb water because water molecules like interacting with the paper towel molecules (cellulose). Water can flow through the paper towel, so it acts as a straw in this experiment. The flow from one flask to the other is powered by gravity. Water flows from the higher flask to the lower one.

I'M **Smart.** get over it!

MCKEYLA MCALISTER

MAKE YOUR OWN GREEN PENNY

LAB SUPPLIES:

- Paper towel
- Petri dish or small shallow, flat-bottomed dish, or the cap from a jar of peanut butter!
- Vinegar
- Penny
- Something flat to cover the dish

INSTRUCTIONS:

Fold a small paper towel a few times so that it fits in the bottom of the petri dish. Pour in a little bit of vinegar so that the paper towel is soaked. Put the penny on the paper towel and cover the petri dish with a lid. Take a look at the penny every few hours and see what happens! Keep the penny in the dish for one day for the best results. Try the experiment using another coin, such as a nickel or a dime. Do you get the same result?

PICKING UP S.T.E.A.M.

with Science, Technology, Engineering, Art & Math:

The surface of a penny is made of copper, a shiny metal. Over time, copper tarnishes and turns green! The Statue of Liberty was originally a shiny copper color, but over time it turned green because its surface slowly reacted with the air. To speed up this process, we used vinegar, which contains acetic acid. In this experiment, the acetic acid reacts with the copper to form a harmless green coating on the penny.

NAILED IT!

CAMRYN COYLE

GO ICE FISHING

- Jar
- Water
- A few ice cubes
- Table salt
- String

INSTRUCTIONS:

Fill two-thirds of the jar with water and add ice cubes. Sprinkle some salt on top of the ice cubes and lay the string on top of the salted ice cubes. Wait about a minute. Then lift one end of the string and see how many ice cubes you "caught." How many ice cubes do you catch if you don't add any salt? Give it a try!

PICKING UP S.T.E.A.M.

with Science, Technology, Engineering, Art & Math:

Fishing for ice may sound impossible, but you can do it with science. The bait is salt, which melts ice. This is the reason why we sprinkle it onto roads in the winter. In this experiment, adding a bit of salt slightly melts the ice at the surface where you put the string. Because we use so little salt, the cube refreezes and now the string is frozen to the ice cube. It's hooked!

STAND Back... i'm trending.

BRYDEN BANDWETH

MAKE YOUR OWN MORPHING STRAW

LAB SUPPLIES:

- Clear jar
- Cooking oil
- Drinking straw

INSTRUCTIONS:

Fill half the jar with oil. Put the straw into the jar until it reaches the bottom and push it to one side of the jar. Bring the jar up to eye level. Look at the straw as you turn the jar slowly, and see what happens to the straw's appearance. How does it change? Can you even make part of it disappear? See what happens if you fill the jar with water instead of oil!

PICKING UP S.T.E.A.M.

with Science, Technology, Engineering, Art & Math:

If you have ever looked at yourself in front of a funky-shaped mirror, you may remember a funny, distorted image. This happens because the light reaching your eye has been bent. In this experiment, a jar filled with oil acts like a lens or a distortion mirror and bends the light reflected off the straw when it passes from the oil into the air. Sometimes the light bends completely in a different direction and it will look as if the straw in the oil has disappeared!

PRETTY BRILLIANT!

ADRIENNE ATTOMS